WHERE WE BEGAN

JORDAN MARIE

Where We Began

JORDAN MARIE

There are moments in life when a good thing comes along at the wrong time.

Juniper Sellers definitely fits that description.

I'm not ready for her, but damn do I want her.

She's a beautiful bird with a broken wing and that spells nothing but trouble.

I'm not strong enough to walk away. I should, because I'm as broken as her.

She's fire and sass.
I'm a moth drawn to her flame.

It's a toss up which one of us will get burned first.

JUNIE

"$\mathcal{I}$'ve got you, Honey. I've got you," he croons.

Embarrassment floods through me. I don't want anyone to see me like this. I'm trying not to cry. I learned a long time ago that when you let a man see you cry that it only gives them what they want. But, when the sheriff puts his shirt over my naked body, and speaks with kindness in his voice, the tears I've managed to hold at bay sting my eyes. I blink them back, but there's no way to stop from crying out when he picks me up.

"Shit, I'm sorry, Junie," he whispers.

Until right in this moment, I never realized that he even knew my name. There's no reason he should have. I'm new in town and the only ones I've really talked to are my brother and his girlfriend.

And my nephew.

I attempt to look over at them, but my vision is so blurry, I can't make anyone out.

"Jo…Joshua," I manage to whisper, my throat feeling as if I've been crawling on the desert sand for days without water.

"He's good, Junie. Let's just get you safe and then I'll go get the asshole who did this to you."

Shame.

That's the overwhelming emotion that fills me. The sheriff thinks that nut-job raped me. He didn't, not completely at least, but what he did was vile enough. I feel dirty in ways that I'm not sure I'll ever feel clean again.

I'm quiet as the sheriff navigates the rubble of this place. My eyes are closed because my head is pounding, and even if they're open, I can't see much. One is almost completely swollen shut, and I'm not sure about the other one.

I'm in shock. I know that. I don't even remember the sheriff undoing my bindings. I have no track of time or space, anything. I keep thinking this is a nightmare that I'm just going to wake up from.

"Get a fucking ambulance here now. I'm pretty sure she has a concussion. I also think her arm is broken, and there's definitely something going on with her hip. I don't want anyone around her but Officer Crane," the sheriff growls.

"I don't..." I whisper the words, not on purpose, it's just that I don't have much of a voice.

"Shh... It's okay, Junie. I'm going to put you in the squad car, but Officer Crane is going to stay with you. She'll be with you even when the paramedics check you out and take you to the hospital."

"She?" I ask, grasping on to the one thing that means the most right now.

"Julie Crane. She's one of my best. You can trust her, Honey."

"Thank... Thank you," I tell him, wishing I could see him, but also grateful that I can't. I don't have to see the pity on his face this way.

"I'll be back, Junie. I'll go to the hospital with you," he says shocking me. I start to tell him that it's okay, that he doesn't need to. I'm wondering if it will hurt his feelings if I tell him that I don't want him there. By the time I get ready to try and explain that to him, he's already put me down on a seat. "Watch her closely," he orders.

"Got it," a woman's voice answers, and I squint enough through my semi-good eye to make out a form behind the sheriff with red hair.

Then, something happens that tilts my world on its axis. The sheriff leans down and kisses the top of my head.

Who does that?

A mother to a child she cares about maybe, although I've never really experienced it. I always said that if I ever had a child that I'd be that kind of parent. I don't see me having children though. I don't know anything about being a parent, and I have horrible taste in men. Tennessee taught me that if nothing else.

"This is Steve, he's the paramedic, he's going to check you out now, is that okay, Ms.?"

"Sell... Sellers," I croak out. "It's okay. I uh... I can't see very well."

"That's all right, Ma'am. We'll get you all fixed up," the man promises. As he starts to ask me about where I'm hurting and explaining what they're going to do, I find myself missing the sheriff's soothing voice. There was something calming about him that didn't make me feel so lost...

I definitely feel lost right now...

BEN

*I*t burns in my gut like an oil fire.

Luna holding on to Lodge is the last thing I want to see.

This wasn't how it was supposed to go. I was ready to settle down, she was a good woman. We were a good match. She wasn't like some of the other women I've known. She understood that my job wasn't nine to five, and she didn't give me shit over it. She had a son, she had a good job, and she wasn't looking for romantic fairytales.

Except, apparently, she was. Because, Gavin Lodge blew back into town and made sure he saved the day and claimed the girl. I'm not even mad. Not really. I'm... jealous.

Damn jealous.

I cared about Luna. We had been dating for a while, I was invested. I trusted her, and I sure as hell didn't expect her to throw me to the side without a backward glance. If I live to be one hundred and three, I'll never understand women. I force myself to look away from her when she stretches up to kiss Lodge.

That chapter in my life is fucking gone. I need to burn the whole damn book.

"Have you heard how Howie is?" Danny, one of my men asks, thankfully tearing my attention away from Luna.

"Waiting for the doctor to come out," I tell him, rubbing the back of my neck. Howie's a good man. Young and green, but a damn good man. I can't help but feel like this is my fault. I still don't know how it happened. We didn't hit anything going into the old school, but Howie and two others were in charge of securing the perimeter, and apparently Atticus, Larry, or fuck who knows at this point, had rigged the back field with explosives to alert them if we tried to sneak in the rear entrance. The other two men were fine, but from what I'm told, Howie's in bad shape. He's in emergency surgery at the moment, and I can't do anything but sit here and wait.

My gaze moves out over the waiting room, and I observe Howie's parents sitting in the corner. The man is holding his wife close and just letting her cry quietly. I feel the weight of her tears. Howie was my man, and I didn't protect him enough. I failed to prepare him for battle on the field, because that's what being a cop is sometimes.

War.

"You did good out there, Kingston. This shit, it's not on you."

I look up at Lodge who has walked over and thankfully Luna isn't with him. I should hate the man, but the hell of it is, I like him. Doesn't mean I don't want to beat the shit out of him every time I see him with Luna.

"I should have made sure they took better care securing the perimeter."

"You were leading the men into the Lion's den. The man had been through training, Kingston," Lodge reminds me of shit that I already know, but don't really give a damn about right now because it doesn't change anything.

"He's barely sworn in," I growl under my breath.

Lodge doesn't have much to say to that. Instead he slaps me on the back in support.

"How's Josh?"

"Good, been through hell and seen shit he should have never seen, but he'll be okay. The doctors are giving him a once over just to make sure."

"How's your sister?" I ask, memories of the pretty blonde who was beaten, violated, and broken still burns in my mind. I doubt the memory will leave me anytime soon.

"If Atticus was alive, I'd kill the bastard all over again," Lodge replies, not really answering my question, but telling me enough, I guess. His sister is in bad shape, and she'll never be the same again. Hell, if his bastard brother was alive, I'd kill him again, too.

The doctor comes out and I turn to watch as he slowly strides over to Howie's parents. I can't hear what he says, but then I don't need to. I know by the way Howie's mother falls against her husband and the howling sound of agony that is ripped from her.

Fucking hell, he's dead...

JUNIE

"*H*ow are you feeling?"

Like someone tried to get me to suck on his pencil dick that smelled like piss and then beat the shit out of me when I refused. Violated because he tried to push the issue.

I don't answer with that. I want to... but I don't.

It's the day after everything went down. I'm still in the hospital, but the doctor says I can get out of here tomorrow, and I'm definitely more than ready for that. I'm not sure where I go from here. Part of me is demanding I load my shit up and get the hell out of Dodge. The problem with that is I'm kind of happy here, or I was until yesterday. I don't really want to skip town. I love being this close to Gavin and to Joshua. I don't want to leave...

I look up to see the sheriff staring at me. I refuse to feel ashamed, but that emotion is there, waiting in the wings. I fight it down. I did nothing wrong. This is not on me. The only thing I did was be a damn magnet for monsters that hide in plain sight...

"I'm fine," I answer, my voice sounding anything but. I avoid the sheriff's knowing look, almost as hard as I'm ignoring the pity in his eyes.

"My grandmother always taught me that when a woman says she's fine, she's anything but."

"Your grandmother sounds like a wise woman."

"Not so much. If she was, she wouldn't have married my grandfather."

"Maybe she loved—"

"Five times."

"Your grandmother married your grandfather *five* times?"

"Five," he confirms, holding his hand up and waving his fingers.

"Maybe your grandmother needed medication?" I suggest helpfully, unable to fathom the idea of marrying the same man that many times.

"That and my grandfather needed to learn to keep it in his pants," he says and just like that, the sick feeling comes back in my stomach.

"Yeah, a lot of people need to learn that lesson," I mutter, feeling the sting of tears, but not letting them go.

"Shit, I'm sorry, Junie. I didn't mean to—"

"You didn't do anything," I tell him, waving off his concern.

"The last thing you needed was some dick bringing up…"

"Dick?" I laugh, trying to make my own joke as Sheriff Kingston continues to put his foot in his mouth. "I'm okay," I insist.

"You've been through hell," he counters and yeah, he's right about that. He's also a little wrong.

"But, I survived," I remind him.

"Junie—"

"Honestly, Sheriff. It was great you coming to check on me, but I'm fine. I've been through much worse than this."

And I had. *I most definitely had.*

"Then you've lived a hell of a life, Junie."

"I can't deny that," I admit and maybe I would have said more but my brother, Luna and Joshua pick that moment to come in.

"Aunt Junie!" Joshua cries making a beeline to me. I barely get my arms open before he hurls his little body into them, and I hug him tightly. I breathe in the goodness that is my nephew, and I do that with my eyes closed, praying some of his goodness rubs off on me, because clearly karma is enjoying making me its bitch.

"Gentle, Josh," Gavin admonishes, but I just squeeze Joshua tighter, refusing to let him go.

"Kingston, what are you doing here?"

I look up when I hear the roughness in my brother's voice. There's a new tension in the room. One I don't fully understand, and I've got a feeling maybe I don't want to.

"Just checking on Junie. I needed to make sure she was okay after all of the shit that went down," the sheriff responds, and he's like a different man now too. Maybe this is Ben Kingston being on duty? I don't know him well enough to understand him, and it's not my place to.

"I can take care of my sister," Gavin growls.

"Didn't say you couldn't," the sheriff replies to this crazy conversation. "Luna, glad to see you're doing okay." He sounds gruff and uncomfortable.

"You too, Ben," she says softly.

"Junie, you take care. I'll check on you again," he promises and then without another word he just leaves.

I just stare at the closed door, but when Joshua pulls away and starts talking animatedly and, thankfully, I happily give him my undivided attention. After everything he's been through he more than deserves that.

I paste on a smile and try to focus on the conversation flying around me. Sheriff Kingston is not my concern and he never will be...

JUNIE

 *ne Week Later*

"I HEAR you're ready to blow this joint."

My eyes jerk up at the door and the Sheriff is standing there. It's not an unusual occurrence. The Sheriff has visited every day to check on me. It annoys my brother, Gavin, to no end. I'm not sure why. I asked him if he was a bad guy and he grudgingly admitted he wasn't. I figure he's just trying to do his job and feels guilty I was abducted and hurt in his town. Maybe that's silly. I've only had a few run-ins with police and they've been helpful, but they can't stop men who are crazier than hell. I've learned that lesson the hard way—and too many damn times.

I squash those thoughts down, locking them away so that I don't think about them. I'm good at compartmentalizing; I could write a book on it. Then, I muster up a smile for my uninvited guest.

"That's what they tell me. I guess you'll be glad," I respond. Truth be known, I'm nervous about returning home to an empty house. I wonder if my doctor realized that because I'm pretty sure he pulled strings to keep me here for so long.

"Definitely glad you won't have to be in the hospital anymore, Junie."

"I meant so you can quit visiting. You don't have to feel guilty about this, Sheriff. It's not your fault. You can't be responsible for a madman."

"That madman was hiding in my county. I can feel guilty about that, Junie."

I shrug. When a man makes up his mind, you're not going to change it. That's another little handy lesson I've learned and relearned.

"Whatever gets you off, Sheriff. Not my problem I guess. I can assure you that I don't blame you, just in case these visits are some kind of penance you are making."

"Not Catholic, Junie. I don't really buy into the whole penance thing. I figure a man does wrong, that wrong is a black mark on him. Nothing he does will clean it off."

I think about that and kind of smile, even though that's still painful. Still, the swelling is gone, and I feel human again, if not a sad, haunted version of a human—but, whatever.

"That's very profound, Sheriff."

"That's me, profound as hell," he jokes, his lips rising a little on one side in a half-assed, lazy smile that I like for some reason.

"Good to know you're not just a pretty face," I tease him, leaning back on my pillow. I've got a headache at the back of my eyes and it just seems to be getting worse, despite the medication the doctor gave me.

"You think I have a pretty face, Junie?" he asks. My eyes open and my gaze goes to him instantly.

"I've seen worse," I respond. We both know he's hot. I don't need to reinforce that. The man's wearing his uniform today. It's a beige color and the shirt has to stretch over his muscles. He's got his holster and gun secured on his hip. His dark hair is closely shorn and when he raises his hand, the back of his palm is covered in dark ink that moves past his wrist and disappears under his sleeve. I can't remember seeing that on any cop I've met before, and it's a damn shame, because even though I pretty much have sworn off men going forward, I find it very sexy.

He chuckles a little at my reply.

"You're good for a man's ego, Junie. Keeps him honest."

"Glad I could help," I mumble, my eyes closing again.

"Are you okay?" He asks, concern laced in the words.

"Headache, but I'll be okay."

"I can call the doctor—"

"There's no need. They gave me something for it. It'll be fine once I get home and sleep it off," I tell him, forcing my eyes to open, even if the light hurts.

"What time are they releasing you?"

"I've already been released. Just waiting for my brother to pick me up. He should have been here, he must be running late."

"Actually, that's why I'm here. Lodge—err…your brother, had to fly out to Quantico for depositions today, and Luna and Joshua went with him for moral support. When he found out they were releasing you earlier than they thought… I'm afraid I'm your ride. Probably last choice, but…"

"Why did Gavin have to do depositions? Is my brother in trouble?" I ask, my heartrate intensifying because I couldn't handle it if Gavin got in trouble over this. He has been through so much and he's finally happy. He deserves that happiness. Luna does too and so does Joshua…

Especially Joshua.

Kids should be made to feel protected and loved, not an afterthought that's in the way. Memories of my mother float through my mind, but I ignore them, employing that handy-dandy compartmentalization skill again.

"Nah, the bureaucrats just want to cover their asses since they had a murderer on their payroll."

"I know that having Agent Dern be a traitor has torn my brother up," I murmur, hating that Gavin had to face that.

"He wasn't an agent. As far as I'm concerned, he's worse than Atticus. At least Atticus was psychotic, but Dern was sworn to protect the innocent and to uphold the law. He's scum, pure scum." There's so much emotion in his words that it hurts to hear it... maybe because I know that pain.

"Gavin told me about the man you lost. I'm sorry, Sheriff."

"You can call me Ben you know," he says after a moment of silence and studying my face.

"I like Sheriff. It suits you."

"Howie was a good man. He deserved a full life with his family. He doesn't get that. That's on me."

"No it's not. It's on the men who did all of this."

"And me. I should have watched out for him better, planned for the unexpected."

"You did that as best you could, Sheriff. You're not God."

He goes quiet for a moment and changes the subject. "Are you okay with me taking you home, Junie? I know we don't know each other that well, but I can call Julie to go with us if you want."

"Julie? Is she your girlfriend?"

"Hell no. Julie's old man would kill me if I ever got that thought in my head. She's a deputy. Officer Crane. You met her at... when you..."

"I remember her," I tell him, when he keeps stuttering over his words. He's trying to walk on eggshells with me. It's not completely necessary, but it's nice. The fact he's willing to get a female cop to ride along with us is nice too. "It's not necessary. I'm not afraid of you, Sheriff."

"Good. You don't need to be. I wouldn't hurt you." I smile at his words wondering why I want to believe him as badly as I do.

"Then, how about you get me out of here so I can go home and shower in my own bathroom and sleep in my own bed."

13

"Your wish is my command, m'lady," he jokes, giving a slight bow—at least with his upper body.

I laugh, even though the action is painful.

"From a sheriff to a prince. What else are you hiding?" I ask as I slide off the bed, gingerly. He comes over to help me stand, taking my overnight bag before I have a chance to bend over to retrieve it.

"I can't tell you. Bringing out all my greatness at once does strange things to women," he says with a wink.

"Like makes them run away?" I quip as we walk from the room. The Sheriff shocks me by laughing. It's a good deep from the soul belly laugh that makes me feel a little warm inside.

"Damn, Junie, not sure I ever met a woman who can bust my balls so easily and yet leave me with a smile."

For some reason that sounds like a compliment.

"Stick around, Sheriff, you haven't seen anything yet," I warn him, and I'm rewarded with another laugh just as we walk outside. The fresh air and the sunshine seem unreal to me and I drink it in, despite the headache. I just need to get home. Everything will be better then.

I hope I'm right.

BEN

*T*he inside cab of my truck is quiet. Junie seems wiped. I sneak a look at her and she's leaning her head against the truck window, her eyes closed.

"I hate to bother you, Junie, but you're going to have to direct me where to go, unless you're still living in the hotel?"

"I rented a house on Courtland Street."

"When did you do that?" I ask.

"Recently," she says, but doesn't elaborate, and I don't press.

"Will you be leaving Stone Lake now?" I ask her, when the silence in the cab of the truck seems too much. I refuse to think it has to do with liking the sound of her voice. My head is too messed up over Luna, and Junie has too much to recover from for me to think of her like that in the first place. Which is a damn shame, because I can tell she's a good woman, despite having Lodge as a brother. The thought makes the corner of my mouth lift.

I look over at Junie and her eyes are still closed. She has the longest dark lashes that I think I've ever seen on a woman and they're not fake, but then I get the feeling nothing about her is fake.

"Trying to get rid of me, Sheriff?" she asks, her eyes, a deep crystal blue, opening to stare at me. I gaze back at the road, shaking my head.

"Not at all. Having you in Stone Lake might just pretty the place up."

"Careful, Sheriff. It almost sounds like you're trying to flirt with me over there."

"Maybe I am," I admit.

"I don't want to break your heart, but I'm officially done with men," she tells me. I glance at her again. "My house is that small white one on the end there." She looks relieved pointing at it as it comes into view.

I pull into the driveway, shifting the truck into park. She reaches for the door and I put my hand on her leg.

"Hold up, Junie. Let me get out and check the house, then I'll come back and help you in," I tell her.

"I'm not an invalid, Sheriff," she grouses.

"Didn't say you were, but you are weak and we've had enough surprises, don't you think?"

"Have at it," she mumbles, clearly unhappy, but giving in just the same. I slide out of the truck, my hand automatically going to the revolver at my side. Since this mess happened, I'm probably overly cautious, but I imagine I will be that way for a long damn time. The loss of one of my own hurts like hell.

"Be right back," I promise her, slamming my door after me. I'm around the hood of the truck, walking up her entrance when she yells out from behind me.

"Hey, Sheriff?" she calls, her head sticking out of the window and as weak and tired as she is, it should be illegal for a woman to look that good.

"Yeah?"

"Not to be a smartass or anything," she adds with a pause, making me laugh. "But won't you need these?" She holds her keys out between two fingers, her pinky finger up in the air as she rocks them back and forth making them jingle. I shake my head, walking towards her, holding my hand out, palm up, underneath the keys. She drops them down and she's smirking.

"I think you might just be a smartass, Juniper Sellers."

"Damn, what gave me away?" she jokes with a smile that in no way reaches her eyes, but it does show she has grit. I close my fingers over the keys and walk back towards her door. I find myself wishing I was in the right headspace to show Junie that she shouldn't give up on men. But, I'm definitely not.

I do a walk-through of her house, making sure it's secure. I'm not sure when she moved but there are boxes everywhere, so it couldn't have been long. It's a tiny crap house that needs a hell of a lot of work too. I should talk to Lodge and see if he knows what kind of dump his sister is living in. When I make it back outside, Junie is already standing by my truck, walking to the door, and carrying her heavy overnight bag. I quickly approach her, jogging so I can take the bag out of her hand.

"I thought I told you to stay put, Junie," I gripe, wondering if the woman might just have too much grit.

"Doing what I'm told hasn't much worked for me, Sheriff," she explains, but gives me her bag without complaint.

"I'm starting to sense that you're very stubborn, Juniper."

"That's the great police training you've had kicking in I bet," she sasses, making me shake my head as she struggles to walk up the small steps to her home. I help her as best I can, resisting the urge to pick her up, because I doubt she'd appreciate it.

"Where do you want your bag?" I ask her once we get inside.

"I'd tell you just leave it by the door, but I doubt you'd do it, so put it on the kitchen table. I can unpack it without bending over that way and you can find a way to live with your conscious."

"It's a good thing your ass is cute since your mouth should be a registered weapon," I respond.

"My ass is cute? I told you, Sheriff, I've sworn off on men. You really should stop flirting," she warns, following me to the door after I put her bag down.

"You're too pretty to become a nun, Junie," I tell her, turning back to look at her. I lean against the wall on the outside of her home as she stands there, holding the door halfway closed and staring back at me.

"I also cuss too much to become a nun," she says with a frank honesty that I definitely like. "Thanks for the ride, Sheriff. I appreciate it."

"Anytime. Just call. Do you have groceries?"

"No idea. But I have a phone and I can call Carl's. That's all I need," she says, mentioning the local pizza shop.

"Cliffside delivers and they have a damn good lobster roll."

"I'll keep that in mind. Thanks again," she says, clearly dismissing me.

I start to walk away, but something makes me stop and turn around to look at her.

"You're a hell of a woman, Juniper Sellers, some guy is going to be damn lucky one day," I tell her, partly because of the sadness in her eyes, despite her quick wit, is bothering me. And partly because there's a part of me hating the fact that the man in question won't be me.

Surprise moves across her features.

"Told you, Sheriff, I'm crossing men off my list."

"Going to pinch hit for the other team?" I ask.

"Going to buy stock in batteries," she responds and this time I full out laugh. "Later, Sheriff."

"Later, Junie." I give her a wave over my shoulder, still laughing as I get to the truck. By the time I'm inside the cab and putting the key in the ignition, Junie has closed the door. Hopefully she will be okay, but I need to let Lodge know she's home so he can keep an eye one her. I know she's independent, but that woman is more than a little broken right now.

Someone needs to watch out for her.

JUNIE

 wo Weeks Later

"SHIT, Junie. I don't want you working there."

"Tough luck, Gavin. I hate to be the bearer of bad news, big brother, but you're not the boss of me."

"The boss of me? Are we four now?" His response makes me smile into the phone receiver. I'm lonely. I'd never admit it, but I miss having Gavin, Luna and Joshua around. They're still in Virginia, and Gavin is *not* happy about it. He's been giving depositions and going through his back cases that he shared with Dern. I know my brother pretty well, and I'm almost positive that he's three steps away from going postal on a bunch of them if they don't let him come home soon.

"Whatever. How are you guys?"

"Trying to make the best of it. We had a couple of days off so we took Joshua to Virginia Beach. I have to head back in tomorrow. It should wrap up this week though. Are you sure you're okay?"

"Will you quit worrying? I'm fine, I swear. I'm a tough chick," I half lie. There was a time in my life that I was tough. Now, I don't feel tough at all. I feel broken, but I'd never let anyone see that. If there's one lesson my mom taught me it's that the minute you show weakness that's the minute you get punched in the lady balls.

"Junie, I know you. I also know that Luna is still having nightmares and she didn't suffer half of the hell you did."

"I don't want to talk about it, Gavin," I tell him, my voice hard.

"Junie—"

I cut him off. I appreciate he wants to help, but I'm not in the mood. "I mean it. I don't ever want to talk about it. It was bad, it was disgusting, and it marked me in ways that you can never understand, because I'm not sure I do."

"Fuck, Junie. I'm so sorry."

"I am too, but we aren't responsible and honestly as contrived as it sounds, it could have been much worse. I'm still standing and Atticus isn't. That's what counts. I'm not about to let him win and steal my life from me."

"I love you, Junie."

"Love you too, Gavin. Can we let this go?"

"I still should be there to check in on you."

"Your guard dog is doing a good enough job. He drops by checking on me at least twice a week." I roll my eyes thinking about the persistence of Sherriff Ben Kingston.

"My guard dog?" Gavin asks, sounding surprised.

"Yeah, the Sheriff. Did you think that I wouldn't know you were sending him out to check on me? I mean I understood it at first, but I've been out of the hospital for two weeks now. Quit worrying and stop asking your friends to check in on me. The Sheriff is nice and all and even kind of cute in a I-wouldn't-blind-fold-myself-if-he-was-in-my-bed kind of way, but honestly I just need some time to be alone and heal."

"Kingston has been coming around your house?" Gavin growls.

Ut-oh. Seems I misread that little nugget of info.

"You haven't asked him to?" I question him, unable to hide my surprise.

"I sure as hell haven't. You stay away from Kingston, Junie. He's bad fucking news."

"Duh, he's a man, I already figured that out."

"I'm a man," Gavin laughs.

"Yeah, but you're my brother. It doesn't count."

"Just stay away from him. I'll call him and make sure he backs off."

"You will not. I'm a grown woman. I can handle my own life, Gavin."

"Yeah, but—"

"No buts. I'll deal with the Sheriff. I would have already, but I thought he was just doing what you asked."

"Junie—"

"Let it go, Gavin. Listen, I love you. You have a good time with your family and stop worrying about me."

"Junie—"

"Gavin, I'm going to be late for work," I remind him of something he already knows.

"I don't want you working at a bar."

"It's not a bar. It's a lounge in a hotel. And I have to pay the bills."

"Not like this. I'll wire you some money."

"I *have* money. Seriously, will you stop? I'm a bartender. This job is how I make my living and have for a while now."

"You need time to heal, Junie."

"Gavin, I love you, but if I sit around this house and listen to the walls for another minute, I'm going to go insane."

"Walls don't make noises, Junie."

"That's my damn point! I can't stand the silence. I'm looking forward to working. I need to stay busy. So let me, okay?"

"Gavin, let your sister live her life," Luna says softly, close enough to the receiver that I can hear her.

"Yeah, Gavin. Let your sister live her life," I repeat with a smirk.

"I know when I'm beat. I can't win against one woman, let alone two. You promise me you'll take it easy and if it gets too much you'll quit."

"Yes, sir. Thank you for letting me have a job, sir."

"Whatever. I'll call you tomorrow."

"Sounds good. Tell Luna and that nephew of mine that I love them."

"Will do. You stay away from Kingston."

"I don't know. Now that I know he's not in league with you to protect me and wrap me up in bubble wrap, I might just take the Sheriff on the ride of his life."

"The hell you will," Gavin growls, and I can't help it. I don't just laugh—*I cackle.*

"Bye, Gavin."

"I mean it, *Junie.* You stay away from that asshole. Don't make me kill Kingston!"

"Later, Big Bro." I click the phone off still laughing.

When the silence of my house invades, the laughter dies on my lips. I wasn't lying to my brother. The silence is slowly driving me insane. I look up at the clock. I don't have to be at work for an hour and it will only take me ten minutes to get there.

I listen to the empty silence in the room one last time and grab my keys. I'll just be early. Bosses like that kind of thing...*Right?*

I make it to the door and turn around to get the stun gun I ordered off the internet the first night I got out of the hospital. I stick it down in my purse, and then head outside, stopping only to lock the door. Outside, it feels like my skin is crawling. My gaze travels from one spot to the next, without taking time to register anything other than it seems like I'm alone. My heartrate is kicked into overdrive and a fine, cold sweat springs out over my palms, the back of my neck and my forehead. I fight down the panic, hating that I'm feeling it. Then I unlock my car.

First, I use the flashlight app to shine through the backseat to make sure it's empty. Then I get in the front seat and slam the door, locking it almost simultaneously.

I hate feeling like a damn coward, but right now, I'm kind of helpless.

It'll get better. I tell myself. *It'll get better.*

I'm not sure I believe it, but I hope like hell it's true.

BEN

 wo Days Later

"KEEP AWAY FROM MY SISTER."

Gavin's words on the phone earlier today are still ringing in my head and pissing me off more with each minute that goes by.

What a fucking dick-wad. I was trying to do him a solid while he was out of town. No, hell, it wasn't even like that. Junie is alone and she needs someone to look after her. If Lodge wants to be a dick, that's one thing. The fact that Junie went crying to him about it is another. This is the first complete night I've had off in what seems like a year. I should be out enjoying myself, not spending it pissed off at Lodge yet again. He got Luna, does he think he can tell me what women are off limits in his world now?

I'd like to think the reason I'm spending my first Friday night off in forever at the local hotel bar is just to piss off Gavin Lodge. I know better. Something about Juniper Sellers keeps bringing me back to her, every single time I walk away. I don't know what it is. Maybe the fact that she's vulnerable and yet still appears hard as nails. Maybe it's that she's witty, smart, and pretty as hell to look at. Or maybe it's just that I haven't been laid in so long I'm not even sure my dick still works, and she's the first woman who's caught my eye since Luna threw me to the curb.

If that's the reason, it'd be stupid. Junie might not have been raped in the traditional sense of the word, but she was violated, and you'd have to be completely blind not to see those scars on her. She's also Lodge's sister and despite maybe that making the perfect revenge on that asshole, she deserves better than to be my rebound sex. No, anyway I look at this, it would be crazy to keep putting myself in Juniper Seller's world...

Yet here I am.

She works the bar like a total pro. You can tell she's had this kind of gig before and often. She's probably the smoothest I've ever seen. Hell, she's better than Elaine was and that woman worked in her bar since she was old enough to sell alcohol. Junie's dressed in a completely black leather outfit that looks as if it's molded onto her like a second skin. Her long blonde hair hanging loose and wavy makes a man want to wrap his hands in it and take her—and knowing her history, just thinking that is enough to send me to hell.

If I wasn't already going there.

I see the exact moment she spots me. She looks up, surprise moving over her features and then she shakes her head as she laughs. Fuck, but she really is beautiful. Now that I'm discovered, I leave the table and make my way to the bar—a bar, that by the way, has become ten times more crowded than normal with the new bartender in question.

"Sheriff," Junie says with an easy smile that doesn't really hit those beautiful blue eyes she sports, but it's more genuine than any I've seen her give here tonight, so I'll take it.

"Junie," I respond, sitting down on the single empty stool that remains. Yeah, this place has become a lot more crowded. Some of these assholes I don't even recognize, and I know everyone in

Stone Lake, which means she's already attracting notice of the guys in the next county over. Then again, that's probably nothing new. I bet Junie attracts guys anywhere she goes, like moths to a flame. Too bad for her that one of those moths was a shit-for-brains, serial killer with even more twisted friends. Signs of her attack have disappeared from her beautiful face, but the shadows are still in her eyes.

"What can I get you?"

"Just a soda."

"Soda? You on duty?"

"Nope, I'm off tonight."

"You don't drink?"

"I do, but I want a clear head tonight so I can escort a pretty girl home from work."

She grabs a glass from under the bar, turns—giving me a great view of the way those leather pants curve over her ass—and goes and fills it with ice and cola. She puts it down in front of me with a coaster under it.

"Don't need you to escort me home, Sheriff. Been driving back and forth without you. I can do it tonight too."

"Didn't say you needed me to, Junie. I said I want to. While we're on the subject though, can I ask you a question?"

"I don't know, can you?"

"Cute," I mutter, shaking my head at her. "You want to tell me why you ran to your brother about me coming over and checking on you? If I was bothering you, you should have just told me."

"Would it have stopped you?" she asks, after studying my face.

"Not in the slightest," I answer honestly, which makes her laugh softly.

"I thought so. But, just to clear the record up, I didn't run to my brother about you checking on me. I told him I was fine for like the hundredth time and then I told him he could call his watchdog off."

"That would be me, I expect."

26

"That would be you," she says, leaning over with her arms folded down on the bar, mostly supporting her. I do my best to ignore the free view of cleavage that gives me. I mostly fail in that effort.

"There's something about me you need to know, Junie."

"What's that, Sheriff?"

"I'm not anyone's lapdog."

"I believe I said watchdog," she corrects me.

"But you insinuated I'd be watching you for him. That would make me his lapdog. I haven't been doing anything other than looking in on a single woman in town who has had a rough time, and making sure someone had her back until she was healed up enough to have her own. I figure that time is pretty close since you're working."

"Then, I guess I should thank you," she responds studying my face.

"Maybe, but let me add this. If *you* want me for a watchdog, all you have to do is say so and for *you* I'd do it, without question."

"Is that a fact?"

"A definite fact."

"What kind of pay does a watchdog get these days, Sheriff? Would I have to feed you treats, or do I scratch you behind the ears? Or, would you prefer I rub your... belly?"

She's flirting, but sill reserved, compared to the Junie who throws sass and gives me hell. She definitely needs someone to have her back still.

Even if she doesn't realize it.

"We could play it by ear, but I am kind of partial to belly rubs."

She laughs, as I intended. A customer waves for her attention and she walks away, still glancing at me.

I don't know what the hell I'm doing, but for some reason I can't seem to leave Junie alone, and I'm going to stop trying...

JUNIE

"*I* can't believe you followed me home," I murmur, as Ben puts one hand against my house and leans over me.

"The way all those men were looking at you in there? I had to. It's my job."

"You're crazy."

"Probably," he says, smiling down at me.

I have my key in my hand, the edges biting against my palm. I should be nervous, but after having the night with Ben sitting at my bar, laughing and talking to him when I could… it's remarkable, but I don't feel nervous at all. I actually feel… kind of safe, which is a completely new feeling to me.

"Are you coming in?" I ask, and I might feel safe, but I'm a little nervous about what inviting him in might mean.

I hate that I feel like this. I'm not this person. I embraced my sexuality a long time ago. I've had men in my bed that I liked, some I cared for, and some I just used to get off and they did the same. Once I got old enough to figure out what I wanted in life, I wanted a committed relationship. I thought I found that in Granger. I truly did. At first it was awesome, but it sure as hell didn't stay that way and I stayed in that relationship longer than I should have. I left him behind only to come here and have some pencil dick rip off my clothes and try to make me suck him off. I didn't let him willingly, and it never got very far because the harder he punched the harder I'd bite when he tried. Eventually he hit so hard that I blacked out and he couldn't have what he wanted before Luna arrived.

There's this huge part of me that wants to let Ben inside to use him. Take him to bed, use him to forget what happened, and to erase the memories of that day with memories of him. A woman would be insane not to know that Ben Kingston would be able to rock her world in bed. It emanates through every pore the man has. Hell, if my brain wasn't so fucked up, I'm pretty sure he could give me an orgasm just by looking at me. He's that intense. That sexy.

"If I come in there, things would happen that I'm not sure either of us is ready for."

"Maybe not, but I'm betting it would be fun."

"Oh yeah, that's a given," he rumbles. His voice vibrates, waking areas of my body up that have been dormant for way too long.

"You definitely know how to make a woman ache, Sheriff."

His hand moves along the side of my face, his thumb brushing against my skin.

"Glad you think so, Junie. Damn glad."

"I think this is the nicest brushoff I've ever received," I whisper, looking up into his dark eyes.

"Make no mistake, Junie. This is not a brushoff. I'm completely available to be the man who eases that ache you're feeling whenever you're ready."

"That's a mighty fine offer, Sheriff."

"I have a name, you know," he says, his lips spreading into a smile that makes me tingle, especially this close up.

"Oh, I know," I tell him, and I do. Tonight is the first night that I've actually thought of him as Ben the man, however, instead of the sexy sheriff checking up on me because of who my brother was. Still, no need to let him know that. I got a feeling that things might come too easy for him. I like making him work for it.

My reply makes that smile on his beautiful lips deepen and those dark eyes sparkle. I could get lost in those eyes. A small wave of panic hits me, and I try my best not to tense up when his head dips and he moves to kiss me. He surprises me, because at the last minute he doesn't kiss my lips... he kisses my cheek. His mouth brushes gently along my cheekbone and then he whispers into my ear. "I'll see you tomorrow, Junie."

"I'll be looking forward to it, Sheriff," I reply, my voice breathy.

He pulls away, and I watch him walk toward his vehicle. He only looks back once, over his shoulder, but he's still smiling at me, and I feel the insides of my thighs dampen even more.

I might not be sure I'm ready, but when it comes to a certain sheriff, my body seems to think I am.

I unlock my door and go inside. Leaning against the door, I pause to catch my breath. I reach over and turn on the lamp on the table by the door and wait for my knees to begin to feel like something besides Jell-O. When I hear Ben drive off I smile.

If a girl has to have a watchdog, he's definitely a good choice...

BEN

"You ride?" Junie asks, surprised.

"Nah, I just like sitting on this thing because it makes me look cool." I don't bother hiding my smirk as I adjust my sunglasses and look up at Junie. She's standing on the top step at her house. Her hair is pulled up in a messy bun, she has a white t-shirt on that has short sleeves that are covered in a camouflaged pattern of green, beige and grays. It's cute, but nothing I would notice, but the little pink skirt she's wearing has definitely caught my eye. It barely covers her thighs. It's pink and glittery and the type of skirt a ballerina would wear when dancing. I take a look down at her feet just to make sure she's not wearing those shoes with the ribbons up her calves. I don't know if I'm pleased or disappointed when instead she's just wearing pink glittery flip flops.

"Well, I hate to admit it, but it does kind of make you look cool."

"Gee thanks."

She shrugs. "I always try to be honest."

"You want to go for a ride?" I ask. My old bike is not much to

31

brag about, but it runs good and I really want Junie on the back of it.

"If I don't go to the store, I'm going to starve to death, Sheriff. There's nothing in the house."

"Go to the store tomorrow. I'll buy you dinner today."

"Well an offer like that is something I can't refuse," she laughs. "Give me a second to stow my purse and shit," she says, turning back around to let herself in the house. She stops abruptly and turns around. "Uh... it might be longer than a minute. I should probably change first. So, maybe you should come in and I'll—"

"Don't you dare take that skirt off."

Her eyes go large at my command.

"You like my tutu?"

"If that's what that pink thing is called, damn straight I do."

"Why, Sheriff, I'm starting to see a different side to you."

"What side is that?"

"Not many men notice what a woman wears."

"Junie, baby, when what they're wearing shows off legs like the ones you're sporting, a man would have to be dead from the waist down not to notice and chances are he would even then," I respond and damn if I don't see the pleasure move over her face. I like that even more than I like that getup she's wearing.

"This skirt is not really made for bike riding."

"I'll be careful. You can trust yourself with me, Junie. I'll take care of you."

Her gaze locks onto me with my words. She studies me as if she's trying to gauge the truth in my words. I sit there and let her piece it together. Suddenly, I have the impression Junie was hurt way before coming to Stone Lake. That means experiencing what she did here is twice as horrible. For the millionth time, I wish I could bring Lodge's sorry fuck of a brother back to life... *Just so I could kill him again.*

She disappears inside for a quick minute. When she comes back outside she skips—*skips*—over to me and then gets on the back of my bike like she's a pro. I press her legs against each side of mine and I want to groan. *Christ*. This woman could be lethal to a man like me.

"You ready?" I ask her over my shoulder.

"Born ready, Sheriff," she yells back, making me shake my head. I start it up and maneuver around and we head out on the road.

Junie's hands wrap around me and she curls into my back. The feel of her fingers digging into my stomach feels like heaven. Once she gets settled, her hold loosens and her hands drop back to my hips, and I miss her touch instantly. I resist the urge to pull her hands back up, but only because I'm driving.

We ride around for a while. I'm not sure how long, but I know it's getting late. I pull in a few minutes later to Cliffside Restaurant which is just a small joint, but the food is amazing. Junie is the first one off the bike, looking at me with the biggest grin on her face. Something inside of me feels as if a piece snaps back in place. Since Luna threw me aside, I've felt kind of hollow, but it's impossible to feel hollow when Junie is smiling at you like she just won the lottery.

"That was awesome."

"You want to eat here, or pick up some food and eat it down by the lake?" I ask her, suddenly hoping she chooses the latter because I'd really like time alone with her.

"Do you know I haven't spent time at the lake since I moved here," she confesses.

"Well, I consider it my civic duty to correct that. Stone Lake is beautiful, almost as pretty as you are."

"God that was lame," she laughs as I slide off the bike. I reach out and take her hand, shaking my head.

"It's a good thing my ego is up to the challenge that is you, Juniper Sellers."

"I'm just surprised you managed to get an ego with those weak-ass lines you use," she responds.

"I'll have you know before you came along women fell at my feet, woman."

"Really?" she mocks, acting shocked in an over the top way that makes me want to swat her ass.

"Yes, really."

"Did you trip them?" she asks and I stop walking, looking at her because I didn't expect her to say it and then it hits me that Junie Sellers is not only smart, she's so fucking sassy she makes my dick ache to try and touch her fire.

"One of these days you're going to bust my balls too much, and I'll spank your ass, Junie," I warn her over her laughter.

"Now, you're just threatening me with a good time, Sheriff," she says and now I'm hoping my damn jeans hide the hard-on that Junie's given me without even trying. Thoughts of me bending her over my bike, pulling her cute-as-fuck skirt down and spanking her ass so that my handprint glows on it as I fuck her from behind, are not helping.

JUNIE

"$\mathcal{I}$ don't think there's anything more beautiful than a sunset," I murmur, as I look up at the sky, a beautiful array of pinks, oranges, blues and whites.

"I don't know, I think I'm looking at something more beautiful right now," Ben states, and I pull my gaze back to him.

He's sitting on his bike, slid back on the edge of the seat. I'm sitting on it too, leaning back against the gas tank and the handlebars, facing him, my legs looped lazily against the seat and at his hips.

I think about his words and smile. I don't even care if his lines are kind of silly. I've become jaded to lines, because in my life that's all they've ever been, but I think Ben might actually mean them. At least, he makes me feel like he does.

"This has been a really nice day, Ben. Thank you for dinner and for bringing me out here." I look away from the sky to the lake behind us, the sun's last rays reflecting off of it, and for the first time since I was abducted I feel some semblance of peace. Coming to Stone Lake wasn't a mistake. Gavin might not be home, but he will be in a few days and having him back in my life, and by extension my awesome nephew Joshua and his mom Luna,

I have a family. My first *real* family. It's a good town. It's far away from Granger and my past. It gives me the chance to start over... which is exactly what I want. I can't blame the town for what happened to me. Honestly, if I want to look at it for what it is, my family is to blame and God knows they always have given me hell. That's kind of how I ended up in Granger's arms anyway.

"Where's your mind at, Junie?" Ben asks, his fingers trailing against the side of my neck.

"What do you mean?" I ask, dragging my gaze back to him and my breath catching in my throat as I see the intensity shining in his eyes, even with the waning light.

"You were a million miles away from me," he says. I roll my bottom lip inward, letting my teeth capture it, the top ones raking against the tender flesh. I do this because Ben's hand has moved down to my midriff, pushing my shirt up and out of his way. His fingers move across my stomach, which is mostly flat—except for a small area that betrays my love of ice cream. The tip of his index finger glides over the small rhinestone at my navel.

"I'm right here," I tell him my voice so breathless that it sounds foreign to my own ears.

"Don't leave me again. I want all of you when we're together."

"Now *that* doesn't sound like a line..." I murmur.

"That's because it's not. This is just you and me, Junie."

"Ben..." I gasp as his hands move to my back and he curves my body up, bringing it closer to him. My head goes back against the bike, letting him have his way, despite my nerves.

"That makes twice," he whispers. His lips are so close to my stomach that I can feel his heated breath.

Need shoots through me, heating me from the inside, and firing my blood to the point that I could almost purr with how delicious it feels. My panties are wet with desire. The air around us thick as we're both caught up in this hunger we bring out in each other.

"Two times and it just gets sweeter," he says and his lips barely touch my stomach in a featherlike kiss that feels better than anything I've ever experienced. Anticipation is killing me. I want more. I *need* more. "Two times, Junie."

"Two times?" I ask, breathlessly, just as his lips skim against my navel, and I feel the brush of the tip of his nose.

"Twice you've said my name. I want more of it," he groans as his tongue comes out and twirls around my piercing, his teeth raking against my skin. Chills move through me, a gush of wetness gathers between my legs, and my nipples harden painfully against my bra.

"Ben," I gasp.

"Third times the charm," he growls and he pulls me so that I'm sitting up, facing him. Our lips are so close, his breath almost as ragged as mine. "Third times the charm, Junie," he repeats, his voice graveled, so much texture in it that it feels like a touch. Then, his lips claim mine.

I tense up immediately. I don't mean to. It's the last thing I want to do. I fight through it, pushing the thoughts that threaten to intrude on the moment away. His tongue plunges into my mouth, searching mine and then the panic swallows me. My body becomes rigid. I don't pull away, but I retreat in every other way that matters and Ben can tell immediately. He pulls back, and looks at me, his gaze moving over me. Sharp, appraising, and I hate that I've ruined the moment.

"Too soon," he murmurs.

"Ben, I... I'm sor—"

He puts his finger against my lips, not letting me finish. "Do not apologize, Junie. You never have to apologize to me about this. Understand?" he asks, and tears sting my eyes, but I don't let them fall... not until he kisses the top of my head and then holds me to him, making me feel like he cares...

BEN

wo Weeks Later

It's been a hell of a day. I ran into Howie's mother at the DMV. She blames me for his death. It ended up being an ugly scene while she screamed at me for letting Howie get killed all to try and save my girlfriend. How I didn't watch over him, didn't protect my own men. She screamed over and over, accusing me of trying to play the hero to win Luna back.

I didn't do it, at least not consciously. Was that what I tried to do? Did my decisions kill Howie? Fuck, everything just keeps replaying in my head. I walked away from the DMV feeling bile rise in my throat and my gut twisting over all of the shit that I wish I had done differently.

Then Junie called. I didn't pick up. My head just wasn't in the right place to talk with her. She's another problem I can't seem to sort through, even if she doesn't mean to be. It's just that this game Junie and I seem to be playing is fun, exciting and... *frus-*

trating. So fucking frustrating that I'm not sure I can take much more.

I swear, I'm pretty sure my poor balls have gone past blue and have turned a cold lifeless purple. There are days it hurts to walk. I jerk off nightly to the thought of Junie, but it's not the same.

I want inside of her.

I want her beneath me.

I want her on top of me.

Fuck.

I want her anyway I can get her.

She's given me the all clear sign, but I've always pulled back. Ever since that day at the lake, I'm making a conscious effort to go slow with her.

Just like I did with Luna.

That didn't really work out for me. There's days I wonder had I pushed our relationship if she'd be with me now and not Lodge? I do a lot of second guessing these days. I've mostly let the memory of Luna and what we could have had go. It doesn't mean it's still not painful, because it is. The hunger I have for Junie is different than what I felt for Luna. It may burn out as soon as I get inside of her. I'm not sure, but I like her, and I want more of her. That's all I really know.

We've done our best to keep our relationship private. Neither one of us want to deal with her brother right now. I don't know Junie's reasons, but I know mine. The minute Gavin catches wind I'm sniffing around his little sister, the bastard will show up here, and I don't want to see his face right now. His or—"

"Hey, Ben, I was wondering if we could talk."

My gaze jerks up to see Luna standing at the door to my office. Fuck, it's almost as if the universe is out to get me today. She looks good. She's wearing one of her dresses that she always wears when at work. It's pink and tight across her body, showing just a hint of cleavage. She looks professional and sexy at the same time. Sitting here and looking at her, I can't help but notice that she looks completely different from Junie. She'd never wear that dress. Junie would wear a pink tutu with glitter covered flipflops and her hair up in a messy bun and she'd rock it. Luna wouldn't be caught dead out like that. She likes to look her best. There's nothing wrong with that, but suddenly I realize that the entire time that Luna and I dated, I tried to live up to that. I kept my tattoos hidden with long sleeves when on duty, I never once took her to Elaine's for a drink and to listen to the music. Yeah, she had Joshua, so our dates were different than most in general, but still, it would have never occurred to me to take Luna to a bar. As I think about it, I realize that the entire time we dated that I never once took Luna out on my bike either.

Was I fooling myself this entire time when it came to Luna? Did I ever let her see the real me? Did I try to change myself to fit what she needed?

It's a hell of a time to think of all the loose ends our relationship left in my head, when the woman in question is standing at my door, obviously nervous.

"Luna, it's been a bad day and I—"

"This will just take a minute, Ben, and I... I need to tell you something that I'd just feel better if you heard it from me," she says and I rub the back of my neck.

It would appear that today is just going to get worse instead of better.

"What's going on?" I ask her, figuring the best way to get this done is to let her have her say so she will leave. It hurts to see her. I might be confused, but that much I know. No man wants to come face to face with the woman who kicked him to the curb for another. That shit hurts the ego. Hell, it nearly destroyed mine, despite Junie telling me that it is huge.

At the thought of that, I'd almost smile, except that when Luna walks in, my gaze moves down to her hand and I see it.

A large diamond ring.

Luna tracks my gaze almost immediately, and I see it on her face before she even speaks a word.

"I uh... thought it would be better if you heard it from me first. Ben... uh... Gavin and I are getting married."

Son of a bitch.

JUNIE

I know the exact minute he comes in. The energy around me changes, I'm that in tune to Ben. Immediately, my body comes to life and everything just feels more electric. He walks to the bar, his long legs striding over, eating up the distance quickly. His face is harsh, even for Ben. I frown, because I didn't expect this at all.

The last two weeks Ben and I have gotten closer and closer. We still haven't had sex, but we're doing some majorly heavy make-out sessions. I'm so sexually frustrated I want to cry. My poor vibrator is getting a constant workout every night. I know he's having the same issues, but no matter how much I beg, he doesn't take what I'm freely offering. I know it's because of the way I froze up when he tried to kiss me. I hate that I did that. There's nothing I can do, and I can't even swear that I wouldn't do it again, despite how much I want Ben. The memories are too close to the surface and anytime something even touches my mouth, I kind of freak out. Hell, sometimes the memories flash through my brain when I'm just eating. Still, I want Ben and the past two weeks he hasn't tried to kiss me... at least on my lips. He's touched me and gotten me so close to the edge that I could literally taste my climax. He has to be tired of the wait, and I *know* I'm tired of waiting.

Is that the reason he looks so upset today?

"Hey there, Sheriff," I say, with a smile. I always call him Sheriff when we're in public and it always makes him roll his eyes. Tonight he doesn't do that, and he doesn't smile after. He barely acknowledges the greeting.

"Get me a bottle of Jack," he growls. He's not acting like himself at all, and I know that whatever is bothering him it must be big. I quickly grab him a glass and a bottle, pouring the golden amber liquid into the tumbler and pushing it towards him.

"You okay?" I ask stupidly.

"I said I wanted the bottle," he says instead. "Leave it." I instantly let go of the bottle. He doesn't talk. He quickly downs the glass I poured him and pours another one.

I help a couple other customers and then go back to Ben. He's nursing his third glass by this time and seeing the white-knuckle grip he has on it, my concern deepens.

I lean in close to him, throwing caution to the wind.

"Ben, Honey, are you okay?"

He doesn't answer at first. He drags his gaze from his glass to look at me. I get the distinct impression that even though he's staring straight at me, it's not really me he sees.

"Sweet as sugar, Junie. I'm starting to think I'm as broken as you are," he says, and I do my best not to flinch.

"That's not nice," I murmur. I know I'm broken, and I know that Ben has seen those pieces more than anyone lately. I don't like that he thinks it's cool to throw it in my face.

"It has to be nice if I say it, Junie. Don't you know? I'm Stone Lake's resident nice guy." he laughs, but there's not a trace of humor in his voice.

"Ben—"

"You know what they say about nice guys, Junie?"

"Ben, I think maybe you should stop—"

"They always finish last. They always lose out. I wonder who you're going to kick me aside for?"

"Ben—"

"Tell me, Junie, who are you going to let between those sexy legs of yours when you get tired of stringing old Ben around?" he asks, his honeyed voice anything but sweet. In fact, it feels like a slap. I've been slapped before and this...

This is much more painful.

"Hey, Kurt?" I call out to my co-worker for the night.

"Yeah, June-Bug?"

"Can you take over? I'm done for the night. I'm going to have Tina come on out and start her shift a little early."

"You okay?" he asks. I look at Ben whose is watching me, his face tight.

"Yeah, just tired of fooling with drunks who act like assholes," I respond, not taking my eyes off the Sheriff. I should have learned my lesson before I let my guard down with Ben.

What in the fuck was I thinking?

BEN

I watch as Junie leaves, disappearing through a small door between the bar and where the booths begin. I stare at the door for a minute knowing I've been a fucking asshole to the one person who didn't deserve it. I'm such a dick. I push my glass away from me, throw more than enough money on the bar, and stalk after her.

The room leads to a locker room of sorts, and I see Junie standing in the corner in front of a locker, brushing her hair with so much anger, I worry she might pull herself bald.

"Junie—"

"Get the fuck out of here," she growls so loudly and with so much hate that I jerk back in surprise.

I've fucked up. Jesus, I fucked up so bad. Seeing the anger on her face doesn't bother me half as much as the pain I see etched there. That will haunt me for the rest of my life.

"I'm sorry, Junie. I was an asshole."

"Yeah? Tell me something I don't know."

"It wasn't you, I'd had a bad fucking day and I was just... I shouldn't have taken it out on you."

"You got that right." She's still refusing to look at me and throwing shit back into her locker.

"If you'd just let me explain."

"I don't want you to explain, Sheriff. I'm not your mother, your best friend, your father or your fucking priest. I don't need your explanation, and I don't want your damn confession. You were right. I am broken. I'm much too broken to withstand that dick move that you just pulled out there. It's fine. You want to be a dickhead that's on you but do me a favor and get the fuck away from me, because I'm done," she huffs, so much anger inside of her that she's shaking with it.

She slams her locker shut and as she goes to walk around me I take my hands and brace them on each of her shoulders.

"You need to hear me out."

"You need to take your hands off of me before I knee you so hard they'll be doing emergency surgery to remove your balls from your throat," she threatens.

"You're a vicious woman, Junie."

"You're a fucking asshole," she says, the words punching me despite them being softly spoken.

"I'm sorry, Junie. I swear. I had a bad day and—"

"I don't care—"

"Annnnd," I say drawing out the word, to try and keep her attention. "I know that's not an excuse. I had no right to give you shit, just because I had a bad day. It was an asshole thing to do and you deserve better."

She doesn't reply, she just stares at me, and those blue eyes of hers that I love so much are full of hurt.

"Howie's mom cornered me this morning and..." My hand shakes as I rub the back of my neck, reliving that scene in the back of my head.

"Howie is the man that you lost," she asks and I do my best to focus back on her.

"Yeah. His mom blames me and she's right. Hell, I blame myself."

"Which is bullshit. Was it bad?" she asks and for a moment my eyes close, but then I open them back up and look at her.

"It was bad."

That's all I say—all I can say. Maybe Junie hears in my tone just how bad it was, or maybe she sees it on my face. Whatever the reason, I can feel her body soften under my hold.

"I'm sorry, Ben," she says, her voice gentle, and reaching a hand out to touch my face. I grab it, holding it there for a minute before bringing it down and staring at it.

"I'm the one that's sorry. I shouldn't have purposely struck out at you because I've had shit come at me today," I tell her. I keep staring at her hand, maybe because I'm avoiding her eyes, not wanting her to see something on my face that might betray just how screwed up my head is right now. I flatten her hand out and rub my thumb over it. It blurs in my vision and suddenly I see Luna's hand there with her ring on her finger that clearly says the relationship we had meant nothing and that I wasted my time because she didn't truly care about me.

"Ben?"

That's when I notice I'm holding her ring finger and my grip is not light. I immediately let go and look at her.

"I'm sorry, Junie."

"Is something more going on?" she asks.

I should tell her about Luna. I should let her know how fucked up my head is right now, but I can't seem to force the words out.

"It's just been a bad day," I tell her, which isn't a lie.

"Why don't you come home with me? I'll make you dinner, and we can veg out in front of the tv until our minds go numb?"

"I'm not sure that's a good idea, Junie. My heads not in the greatest of places and you and I have been..." I trail off, because I don't know what we've been doing. I don't know much of anything right now."

"Whatever happens, happens. We're both adults and I think you get by now that I like you. What do you say?"

"Let's make it my place, and I'll order a pizza."

"Afraid of my cooking?" she smiles.

"I want you in my bed tonight, Junie."

"Ben, I—"

"I'm not saying anything has to happen tonight, Junie. I'm just saying that it has been a fucked-up day, and I'd like having you in my bed, lying in my arms as I sleep."

"Just sleep?" she laughs.

"If that's what happens, definitely. No pressure here, Junie. Like you said, we're both adults," I tell her, even as I'm wondering what in the hell I'm doing. Having Junie back at my place tonight is a horrible idea. My head is fucked up over Howie, over Luna and hell, life in general. I need to tell Junie that she needs to find someone else. She's vulnerable, and I don't want to hurt her. *Fuck.* I don't want to let her go either. I shove all of this back, and just focus on tonight. The rest can wait. I don't want to be alone tonight either. Right now, I want someone in my arms that is there because they want to be. Not because I'm a substitute for a love they lost years ago.

Fuck Luna, this isn't about her.

This is about me and what I need for once.

JUNIE

"You're still awake," Ben whispers against my ear, his arm pulling me in tighter to his warm body.

"Not used to having anyone in bed with me," I half lie. That's not why I'm still awake, but I don't know how to explain to him about how bad my insomnia is. I've had it for a while…. Since Granger, really. What happened here in Stone Lake may have made it a little worse, but it's a familiar enemy.

"I like that you didn't leave after dinner and the movie tonight. I like even better that I didn't have to leave you to go out into a cold truck and drive home to an empty bed," Ben says and all that he says is nice. It's not wrong either, because I like all those things.

He's been quiet tonight. It's understandable after his run in today. I know that had to hurt him. I'm trying my best not to hold my resentment at the way he lashed out at me. That's not easy for me, even if I understand. It wouldn't be easy for anyone with my history. It does have me feeling unsettled though, I can't lie.

"I like that too," I finally whisper.

"What are you thinking about, Junie?"

This is it. This is where I decide to let Ben in past my walls, or if I should keep a safe distance. I don't know where we are headed, heck I don't even know if I'm ready for a relationship. But, I do know I like Ben, and he's the first guy that's treated me like I matter—with the exception of Gavin, who doesn't really count because he's my brother.

"Old ghosts," I whisper into the darkness, mostly hoping he lets it go.

I knew he wouldn't. He turns to his nightstand and turns on the light there. It bathes the room is a pale soft light and I'm glad. If it was bright, I'm pretty sure I'd freeze up.

He turns back to me, going up on his elbow and bracing his head on his hand, as he looks down at me. His other hand comes over and lays on my stomach. I watch that hand, not ready to look at his face. His beautiful ink shines bright against the stark white t-shirt—Ben's t-shirt that I'm sleeping in. I run my finger over the ink, tracing it, memorizing it, and delaying the talk I know is coming.

"Tell me about your ghosts, Junie."

"Just ghost really. My family was fucked up, but I hit the road early so they didn't get a chance to leave their mark too deeply," I tell him, glossing over my past. Then again, I'm going to gloss over Granger, too. Ben can fill in the blanks if he wants to, but I'm not talking about it. In my experience, if you poke at the past hard enough, it likes to rear its head and bite you in the ass.

"Okay, Baby, tell me about your *ghost.*"

"There's not a lot to tell, Ben."

"Fuck, I love when you call me Ben," he says, his voice rumbling as he leans down and places a kiss on my nose.

I know he kisses me there because of the way I stiffen when he goes to kiss my lips. The fact that he's trying not to pressure me and is handling me with care means something. I need to let go of the earlier argument. Ben had a rough day. Okay, he was an asshole and he was kind of mean, but he's not Granger. Right now is proof of that.

"I called you an asshole tonight too. Did you like that?" I laugh.

"I believe you called me a dickhead, and I was, so yeah I like it. I like that you called me on my shit and didn't let me get away with it. You're a strong woman, Juniper Sellers."

"God, I hate that name," I groan.

"I think it's beautiful, just like you."

"There you go with your lines again," I mumble.

"It's not a line. None of it is. You are beautiful, breathtaking even. You're also one of the strongest women I've ever met."

"I try to be... I wasn't always strong, so I made a promise to myself that I would never become the naïve kid I once was."

"Is that where your ghost comes from?" he asks and I make the decision to leap and give him the bare facts.

"His name was Granger."

"Granger? Jesus do people where you live ever hear of simple names?" Ben laughs.

I smile despite the memories. "His name wasn't always Granger. It was Greg. He changed it."

"He changed his name? What in the hell for?"

"He wanted to be rich and famous. Wanted to be the next George Strait."

"Oh hell."

"Yeah. I followed him to Nashville. I thought I loved him, but mostly I just wanted away from my crazy-ass mother."

"How old were you?"

"Seventeen and as stupid as they come."

"Damn."

"Yeah," I reply, feeling so stupid even now.

"What happened?"

"I got a job waitressing. Worked at night to get my GED. I didn't mind it. Nashville was a good place."

"What did dickhead Granger do?"

"Dickhead Granger?" I laugh, finally summoning up the nerve to look at him. He's smiling down at me, his eyes kind.

"I decided he needed that name more than I do."

I laugh, letting my fingers go back to tracing his ink.

"It fits him," I murmur.

"I figured. So what did he do while you were working?"

"Wrote music, attended jam sessions to help get his name out there."

"And did it?" Ben asks, and it's comforting that I don't hear judgment in his voice, especially when I mention having to get a GED. I hate that I quit high school. I'm proud of myself for what I accomplished though.

"Believe it or not, yes. Granger was talented when it came to playing the guitar. All of these stars would hear him play and want him on their tracks. He made a lot of money being a musician."

"That's good then, right?"

"I thought it was, but Granger didn't. Every time he got turned down and didn't get a recording contract, he got... mean."

"Fuck, Junie," Ben hisses.

"Yeah."

"Did he hurt you?"

I close my eyes at that question. It's a simple question, and Ben's voice is so soft that it should be soothing, but it is really anything but, because the answer isn't that simple at all. It's definitely not as simple as I make it.

"Yeah."

I wait for Ben to come back with the next question. The same one that everyone asks when they hear my story.

Why did you stay?

It's going to hurt to hear that from him. I could defend myself, tell him I didn't, tell him that I kept leaving and Granger kept coming after me, begging until I took him back. Then when that stopped working—because I was stupid enough to let it more than a few times—he became more...persuasive. Turns out, a woman will go back every time if the threats are good enough.

Ben surprises me though. He doesn't ask that question. He doesn't come at me with judgment. Instead, his hand moves down from my stomach and his fingers hook into the waistband of my panties and he tugs just enough to get my attention.

"What are you doing?" I ask, surprised while looking at him and thinking I'm going to see disgust, but I don't see anything but... *Ben.*

"Showing you that not all men hurt, Junie, even when they can be dickheads," he responds, and his fingers slide deeper into my panties and graze against my clit.

I keep my gaze on Ben completely in shock with uncertainty flooding through me.

BEN

*T*he sadness in her voice and on her face undoes me. I shouldn't have pushed her to tell me about what keeps her from sleeping. Jesus she's been through enough. This is probably the wrong move too, but I want to make Junie feel good. Fuck I want to feel good too. Both of us have had too much shit for way too long—her more than me. If we can find pleasure with each other, then why in the fuck shouldn't we? We're adults. We've definitely been through enough shit that we know the score and damn it, I want her, and I think she wants me too. If she puts a stop to this, then so be it, but if I don't make this move, I know I'll regret it.

"Tell me to stop if you don't want this, Junie," I tell her, giving her the option. I want this to be about pleasure, nothing but pleasure.

"I'm not sure what I'm ready for. I mean, I want this, Ben, I swear. But the memories…"

"We'll go as slow as you want, Junie, and I'll quit the minute you tell me to," I assure her, waiting to see what she does. I watch her and it feels like I can't breathe while I pause to see what her move will be.

She looks up at me and fuck, those blue eyes cut through me. They're so full of emotion, so deep and intense they rob my damn lungs of air. Slowly—so slowly that I'd swear time was coming to a standstill—she lifts her hands and leans up to whisk my shirt over her head. I've teased her breasts through her shirt over the last week when we've spent time together. But, I haven't seen them. I always thought I was an ass man, but looking at Junie's breasts, it's clear I'm definitely a tit man.

Junie's are beautiful. Soft round globes the color of peaches and cream, her nipples pebbled, contracted, and a soft rose in color. I let my finger move over the tip, smiling as it moves with my finger and Junie catches her breath.

"Ben."

I look up at Junie and smile at her. I'm dying to kiss her, but I don't want to do anything to stir those memories she has trapped in that quick-witted brain of hers.

I bend deeper and run the tip of my tongue following the same path my finger just took. Junie's skin tastes sweet like honey, and I can't wait to taste the rest of her. I feel her fingers sifting through my hair, and I suck a nipple deeply in my mouth. I'm rewarded with Junie's groan.

The need to kiss her is so fucking strong. When I finally get to put my lips on hers, I won't let her come up for air. To distract myself, I kiss a path down her stomach, worshipping her body. How anyone could take pleasure in hurting Junie boggles my mind. I've been a cop for a while, I know there are fucked up people out there, but you would think a man who had been blessed with the love of a good woman would do nothing but appreciate it.

I let my tongue flick back and forth against the rhinestone in her navel, then tease her belly button. Her body jerks in reaction, and I look up to find her watching me, her blue eyes smoky with desire, her breath coming quick enough her breasts sway upon exhale. Her face is flushed and she's rubbing her lips together.

"You good, Junie?" I ask her, hooking my fingers once again in her panties.

"I... think so," she answers, her voice steady.

"Lift up for me, Baby," I tell her.

She raises her ass up just enough so I can push her panties down and helps me slide them from her legs and off the bed.

"Jesus, Junie," I literally moan, when I'm left to take in her bare pussy, juices covering the tops of the lips. I inhale deeply, taking in the sweet scent of her hunger.

Before I lose my head, I slide my own boxers down, throwing them on the ground. My cock is rock hard and my balls are heavy. It's been so fucking long, and I can't remember being as turned on as I am right now—which is crazy as hell, because Junie has yet to touch me.

"Are you still okay, Junie?" I ask, checking on her, but finding it hard to talk at the same time.

I need inside of her.

"Damn, Sheriff, you really are packing," she murmurs her eyes wide as she takes in my hard cock.

"Ben," I correct her.

"What?" she asks, pulling her gaze from my cock to look at me.

"When we're together like this, Junie. I'm Ben. Fuck that, to you I'm always Ben."

She smiles, shaking her head, like she thinks I'm funny, but she doesn't disagree.

"Where do you keep the condoms, *Ben?*" she asks and I freeze.

"Fuck."

"No, no, no. Do not tell me you don't have condoms," Junie begs.

"There's been no need.... It's been a while for me, Junie," I tell her, which is the truth. Mine and Luna's relationship had gone slow, so fucking slow sometimes I wondered why it didn't bother me more. Luna was a good woman. I told myself it was worth the wait, and I guess it was—or would have been. But feeling the need

I have for Junie right now, I'm beginning to wonder if that's true. I stop myself from going there. I will not think about Luna when I'm in bed with Junie. She deserves better than that. Hell, I do too.

"Are you on the pill?" I ask hopefully.

"Yes, but... shit, Ben, don't be mad... but..."

I take in a deep breath and flop over on my back, because I understand and she's smart. That doesn't mean I'm not cursing myself. "I would have had condoms, but I just went through kind of a breakup and dumped them in the trash in anger."

"Kind of a breakup?" Junie laughs, her breaths still coming quick, as I pull her to me. She flops a leg over me and my cock bounces in reaction, so hard it's painful.

"She ditched me for another man," I tell her, skirting issues I should probably tell her.

"Ouch, that had to hurt," she says and I sigh.

She has no idea...

"Junie—"

"Most men would have used the condoms to fuck every woman in sight just for revenge, Ben."

"That's not who I am. I didn't want to use those condoms," I tell her, not adding that Luna and I picked those condoms up together because we were planning on taking that step the night a rock was thrown through her window. "I didn't want to use condoms I bought for one woman, on someone else," I tell her lamely. It's mostly a lie. I threw the condoms away because it fucking hurt to look at the box and know what they represented and what happened. I guess we better get dressed..." I murmur, knowing the moment is gone.

"Tomorrow, we'll go buy condoms," she says and when I look in her eyes I nod my head in agreement.

"The sooner the better," I tell her, which makes her grin.

"We could...."

"What?" I ask, liking that look in her eye.

"Fancy a hand job, Sheriff?" she asks.

With anyone else that might be a disappointment, but with Junie, it sounds damn good right now. When her hand wraps around my shaft and she squeezes, it really does.

"I told you that when we're together you call me Ben," I half growl as she holds me tight in her fist and strokes my cock.

"Sorry," she whispers. "You can spank me for it later."

My dick trembles in her hand at the thought of spanking her. She has no idea the stuff I want to do to her. If she did, she wouldn't tease me.

"You may regret giving me the go ahead on that one day, Baby."

"I don't think so," she says, her words breaking off in a gasp as I slide my fingers between the lips of her wet pussy and seek out her clit.

We're staring straight at each other. Her tongue coming out to lick her lips as her hand works my cock. My finger gliding over and over her throbbing little clit. Her thumb moves over the head of my cock, spreading the precum over it. I've already leaked out so much that my shaft is wet, making it so her hand glides easily.

"Are you going to come for me, Junie?"

"God, I hope so," she whispers, and this time she twists her hand on an upward glide and it feels so good that my balls tighten. "Are you going to come for me, Ben?"

"You keep doing that and definitely," I respond.

"I feel like a kid in high school, giving the football jock a hand job under the table in chemistry class," she whispers, her grin deepening.

"Then you better hurry and do your job like a good little girl before the teacher catches us, hadn't you?" I tell her, playing along.

"You'll have to be quiet when you come. If you're not everyone will know that I've been a bad girl."

"Did you really give the football player a hand job in chemistry, Junie?" I ask, as I push two fingers inside of her slick pussy, letting my thumb brush against her clit.

"Yeah, I wanted to see if he could keep quiet."

"Did he?"

"Not even a little. Came really quick too. We broke up soon after that," she says the words in a low sultry tone, her hips rocking as I finger fuck her, thrusting in and out of her, her pussy so wet the slippery slick sounds echo around us.

I'm close to coming, I know it and I'm pretty sure she does if that smile on her lips is anything to go by.

"Fucking loser," I growl, stepping up my game and finger fucking her harder, tunneling my digits in and out of her tight cunt so roughly her hips are jerking in broken movements and a moan escapes her lips, as her heel pushes into my hip. "He could have at least given as good as he got."

"Well," she gasps, her hand moving faster and faster over my cock. "We were in class…"

"Doesn't fucking matter." I exhale bending down to suck her nipple into my mouth, biting the tender skin as I pull my fingers out of her pussy, sliding them against her clit fast and hard.

"What would you have done?" she asks her head going back in pleasure, as I work her clit so hard that I know it will be sore when all this is done. I know it, but I don't care. I want her to remember that my fingers owned her pussy tonight and tomorrow night, my fucking cock will.

I lean up and find her ear, then I nibble around on the shell, smiling as her body shudders against me in reaction. Then I whisper my filthy little story to her, that I can tell she likes because her pussy gushes in reaction.

Christ, I wish I was inside of her.

"I'd have pushed you down against the table on your stomach. Lifted up your skirt, ripped off those cute little cotton panties you wore to tease all the boys, and fucked you hard. So hard the table would scrape against the tile, but you couldn't hear it over your cries for more," I whisper. "And I'd make you beg for me to fuck you harder in front of everyone and every time you did as I asked,

59

I'd reward you by spanking that sweet little ass of yours red, Junie. What do you think about that?"

It's a silly question, I can tell because I can feel her body tighten. She's coming.

"I think that I *really* wish you had been in school with me," she pants, and I can feel my balls tighten. I'm about to blow. I can't hold back, and I don't have the strength to try. I somehow manage to capture her slippery soaked clit and pinch it hard, twisting it. She shatters in my arms, calling out my name, and a second later my cock releases its first jet of cum in rhythm to her hands movement. Then I come again and again, emptying my load against her soft skin.

"Junie," I pant into her ear as I give up the final stream of cum. Her body still quivering curls into mine, and her hand slows on my cock, until it's just a gentle, broken slide, meant to soothe.

"Ben," she responds, saying nothing else, but then that's enough.

More than enough.

JUNIE

$\mathcal{I}$ snuggle against Ben, smiling a smile that I feel all the way in my soul.

This.

This is exactly what I moved to Stone Lake for. I've never experienced anything like what Ben and I shared tonight, but it was beautiful and fun and easy. There was no pressure, he didn't try to kiss me, and I saw the way he looked at my lips, he wants to. The truth is, I want him to kiss me too. I think I'd be okay, and we'll try it tomorrow. For the first time in a long time, I'm looking forward to tomorrow. This thing with Ben is definitely new, and I know I have a lot of healing to do, but I'll get there. I have a very good feeling about Ben, and after everything that I've been through, that's no small feat.

I kiss his shoulder and squeeze him. My eyes are finally beginning to feel heavy. Ben fell asleep an hour or so ago, holding me tight to him. I've never had anyone do that before. It feels nice... like I matter.

"I know you're asleep, Ben. I probably wouldn't tell you if you were awake, I wouldn't have the nerve. But, tonight is one of the best nights of my life. Thank you for being you." I whisper all of that against his ear. I do it slowly, and as quiet as possible, because I really don't want to wake him. It's just my heart feels so full right now.

"Luna," he whispers and I blink. Surely, I misunderstood him.

"Ben," I question, though my voice is barely more than a breath —a painful, frozen breath that I have to force out of my lungs.

"Luna, kiss me," Ben says, his head burrowing against the side of my neck, his nose brushing against my flesh.

I think back over our conversations.

Recently suffered a bad break up. She ditched me for another man.

I could be jumping to conclusions, but when I think about it, it all clicks into place. Including the way my brother and Ben seem to dislike each other without a real reason.

Then, the final piece in the puzzle clicks into place with a giant smacking noise echoing in my brain. Earlier today, Gavin told me that him and Luna are officially engaged now. When I told him to put Luna on the phone so I could congratulate her, he told me she was gone because she wanted to tell her ex before he found out about it from other people. Gavin wasn't happy about it, but let her go, because Luna wasn't going to let him convince her she shouldn't.

Suddenly Ben's entire attitude makes a lot more sense. Especially when I remember how he asked me who I was going to kick him aside for. Pain rips through me, unlike any I've felt before, because this pain comes with so much anger it's physically hard to contain.

I don't think, I just react. I get up and walk into the bathroom. After Ben and I cleaned up earlier I put his shirt back on. I rip it off over my head and throw it on the floor, finding my old clothes that I wore from work tonight. I put them on quickly and just before I'm about to leave I notice a large bowl on the sink counter. I grab it and put it under the bath faucet. It's taking too long to fill, so I end up shutting it off when the bowl gets one-half full of cold water.

I flip the bedroom light on and then carry the water over to the bed, looking down at an unsuspecting Ben—the asshole. Then, I just turn it upside down, drenching him.

"What the fuck!" he growls, jumping up in the bed, looking around trying to figure out what just happened. His eyes light on me and confusion is clear to read, despite the water streaming down his face, as he pushes his hair away.

"Junie? What in the hell is going on?"

"It's good you know my name. I guess you just have to be *awake!*"

"What are you talking about? Junie, this isn't funny. Did you forget your fucking meds today or something? Jesus, why am I always getting messed up with women who have fucking issues?"

"You mean like, Luna?" I growl and that's when Ben goes still, there's a light going off in his head, I'd bet money on it.

"Junie..."

"The girl who dumped you for another man, Ben. Was it, Luna?"

I don't know what I expected from him. Maybe I hoped he'd deny it.

He doesn't.

"Yeah, Junie. It was Luna."

"You love her," I whisper, feeling something that had just sparked into life die inside of me.

"Yeah, maybe... or maybe not. Hell, Junie, I don't even know anymore. It's confusing," he says with a brutal honesty that probably wasn't meant to hurt me, but does all the same.

"I tell you what's not confusing, *Sheriff.*"

"Junie—"

I keep talking over his pathetic attempt to backpedal. "The fact that you called me *her* name in your sleep."

"Damn it, Junie, just let me think here."

"And you did that within an hour of me getting you off."

"Junie—"

"No, not Junie. Only people who are important in my life call me Junie, Sheriff. That's definitely not you. Not now," I tell him and then I walk away.

Ben doesn't even try to stop me, which just goes to show what an idiot I truly am, because I spend the entire time wishing he would...

LIKE WHAT YOU'VE READ? Ben and Junie's story will wrap up in Before We Fall, now available for preorder. For more information click here:

Before We Fall

PROLOGUE

ONE YEAR LATER

*J*uniper Sellers has trouble written all over her. I knew it the first moment I met her, and I should have made it my mission to ignore her. But, it's not easy to ignore a woman who looks like Juniper. She's so damn hot that she should come with a warning label. The woman has curves that go for miles, legs that were made to wrap around a man and give him the ride of his life, and lips so sweet they fucking haunt me.

I was drawn to her from the beginning, even though I knew I should have run in the opposite direction. I didn't, even knowing I wasn't ready, and then I fucked up. I freely admit it, and I did it in one of the worst ways a man could. There's no going back from it now and you would think that would be enough to make me give up and walk away.

Instead, I'm sitting on this barstool, nursing a whiskey and watching every move she makes. I've watched every man in this damn place flirt with her. Watched her laugh and shoot every single one of them down.

A woman who looks like her could have her choice of any man she wants but the more attention she gets, the more she pulls away. That's proof she's still broken. Proof she needs a man at her back.

Regret is a fucking bitter pill to swallow.

I want to push my way back into her life. Wrap my hands into that beautiful silvery-blonde hair of hers and claim those lips that haunt my dreams.

I want to do a lot more than that to her.

And that's a problem.

Juniper Sellers is the last woman I should be attracted to. The last woman I should want. Her brother Gavin Lodge is a thorn in my side. I hate him—and I like him. It's definitely a confusing relationship, and if he knew I was dreaming nightly of fucking his sister, while jacking off to my hand... *He'd fucking lose it.*

"Sheriff, did I forget to pay a parking ticket or something?" the object of my obsession asks, surprising me.

"What do you mean?" I cock a brow up at her while shooting her a smile because I like her style. Not many women will call a man on his shit. I like that Juniper doesn't even hesitate.

"If you stare at me any harder you might hurt yourself."

"It's a good view, Juniper." She winces as I say her full name— just as I knew she would.

"Listen, Sheriff. I don't mind being your eye candy, but can you *not* call me Juniper?"

"That's your name, right?"

"June. Call me June."

I grin even though I don't want to. "June it is," I tell her, raising my whiskey up and waving it at her before taking a sip.

"Whatever. You're an odd bird, aren't you?" she asks, shaking her head.

"Are we on for tomorrow, Junie?" Clyde Short calls out, taking June's attention away from me.

"Yep, we're closed for the next three days, Clyde. If you could spray and crap then, you'll be my hero."

Juniper bought Elaine's Tavern a little over a year ago. She did

66

a fuck of a lot of renovations, and I have to admit the place looks sweet. It's been hopping ever since it opened too, despite Juniper still having a few things left to do to the place—one of which apparently is exterminating. Of course she's opening a kitchen in the back, so that makes sense.

"Now, that's something to make an old man's heart twitter-pate," Clyde says, and I roll my eyes at seeing the old asshole flirt with her. He's old enough to be her grandfather.

"Twitterpate?" she laughs. "Is that healthy for a man your age, Clyde?"

"Honey, at my age if it feels good you do it. To hell with healthy."

"Point made. What time do you want me here?" she asks.

"I'll be here at eleven. I've got to clean out my old lady's crawl-space before I come spray yours."

"You're going to be a busy man," she laughs.

"Yeah, but one of those will be a hell of a lot more fun, and I won't have to smell chemicals, just sweet woman."

"That's the horniest man this side of the ocean," I mutter.

"Jealous?" Juniper asks.

"Why would I be jealous?"

"I'm just saying, he's going home to his woman, not sitting alone at a bar on a Friday night nursing a whiskey."

"Nothing wrong with my parts, I just don't happen to have a woman at home. Now, if you'd like to volunteer for the position for the night..."

"Not on your life, Sheriff. I bought that damn t-shirt and learned the hard way not to tangle with the law."

"Now that's a shame, Juniper."

"You keep calling me Juniper those working parts you're bragging on will be in danger of permanent harm," she says softly.

"You don't want to do that," I tell her, and I watch as her tongue darts out on her lip nervously as she looks into my eyes.

"Why not?"

"Because one day soon, Juniper Sellers, you're going to like my *working* parts."

"You are dreaming, Sheriff Kingston," she responds, her gaze narrowing, and I know I'm pissing her off. The thing is, I like when I piss her off. Hell, I like everything when it comes to Juniper, except the fact she's not warming my bed.

"We'll see," I tell her, enjoying our cat and mouse game.

"Do I look stupid to you, Sheriff? Because I promise you I'm not," her voice drops down and she leans into me so I can hear her over the loud music and voices surrounding us.

"Never thought you were, Junie," I tell her, and she flinches when I use her nickname.

"June. Only people I care about call me Junie."

"You let me call you that once," I remind her.

"I did, but you didn't call me Junie when it mattered, did you Sheriff Kingston?"

She walks away after that, and fuck me if I don't watch her ass sway as she goes, holding my glass so fucking tight it's a wonder it doesn't shatter in my hand.

Yeah, I definitely fucked up with Juniper Sellers.

I watch her until I finish my drink. Juniper never does come back. Instead, she sends a waitress over to take care of me instead. I'm okay with that because I know sooner or later Juniper and me are going to tangle with one another again.

Nothing will stop it...

More about this book can be found here:
Before We Fall

JORDAN'S EARLY ACCESS

Did you know there are three ways to see all things Jordan Marie, before anyone else?

First and foremost is my reading group. Member will see sneak peeks, early cover reveals, future plans and coming books from beloved series or brand new ones!

If you are on Facebook, it's easy and completely free!

Jordan's Facebook Group

If you live in the U.S. you can **text JORDAN to 797979** and receive a text the day my newest book goes live or if I have a sale.

(Standard Text Messaging Rates may apply)

And finally, you can subscribe to my newsletter!

Click to Subscribe

SOCIAL MEDIA LINKS

Keep up with Jordan and be the first to know about any new releases by following her on any of the links below.

Newsletter Subscription
  Facebook Reading Group
  Facebook Page
  Twitter
  Webpage
  Bookbub
  Instagram
  Youtube

Text Alerts (US Subscribers Only—Standard Text Messaging Rates May Apply):

Text *JORDAN* to 797979 to be the first to know when Jordan has a sale or released a new book.

Craved

Burned

Released

Shafted

Beast

Beauty

Filthy Florida Alphas

Unlawful Seizure

Unjustified Demands

Unwritten Rules

Unlikely Hero

Doing Bad Things

Going Down Hard

In Too Deep

Taking it Slow

Lucas Brothers

The Perfect Stroke

Raging Heart On

Happy Trail

Cocked & Loaded

Knocking Boots